This book belongs to:

A catalogue record for this book is available from the British Library

Published by Ladybird Books Ltd
80 Strand, London, WC2R 0RL
A Penguin Company

2 4 6 8 10 9 7 5 3 1
© LADYBIRD BOOKS LTD MMVIII
LADYBIRD and the device of a Ladybird are trademarks of Ladybird Books Ltd

ISBN: 978-1-84646-928-2

Printed in China

My Storytime

Daisy
Learns to Dance

written by Marie Birkinshaw
illustrated by Simona Dimitri

Daisy loved to dance. More than anything else she wanted to be a famous ballet dancer. Every night she dreamed of performing in front of a real audience.

Today was Daisy's first lesson at her new dancing school. As she walked into the huge hall, she felt a bit worried.

"Hello Daisy," said Mrs Pringle, the dancing teacher. Daisy thought Mrs Pringle looked beautiful – elegant, tall and graceful.

Then Daisy met the rest of the class. They had all been to the ballet school before. Daisy was the only new one there and she was by far the smallest dancer in the hall. Now she began to feel very worried indeed.

Daisy looked around at the other dancers.
They were warming up, ready for the
lesson to begin.

She could see Selina and Sophie,
admiring themselves in the mirror. They
were so tall and slender. Then there was
a group of dancers exercising at the barre.

Suddenly, three boys came rushing across the room and knocked Daisy over. They were the Noisy Trio, as Mrs Pringle called them – Jack, Dan and Andrew.

"Whoops! Sorry!" Jack said to Daisy. "You're so small, we didn't see you."

"Listen now, everyone!" called Mrs Pringle. "This summer I would like the class to perform The Silver Swan, and you will all take part."

Everyone cheered. They had all heard of The Silver Swan. The costumes were great, and the music was brilliant with lots of drums, trumpets and tinkling chimes.

Daisy wasn't sure what it was, but she felt excited all the same.

"This morning," said Mrs Pringle, "I am going to choose who will play each part. We will start with the trees. Listen to the music and watch carefully!"

Mrs Pringle waved her arms and danced on the spot. She looked just like a beautiful tree swaying in the breeze.

Swish! Swish! Swish! Swish!

"Now it's your turn!" said Mrs Pringle.

The dancers waved their arms and danced on the spot.

Swish! Swish! Swish! Swish!

Mrs Pringle chose Selina and Sophie to be the trees... but she didn't choose Daisy.

"Next," said Mrs Pringle, "I want you to dance like fire! Listen to the music and watch carefully."

Mrs Pringle danced towards Selina and Sophie. Her arms leapt out, like fiery flames around slender trees.

Flicker! Flicker! Crackle! Crackle!

"Now it's your turn!" said Mrs Pringle.

The dancers leapt round the hall like raging fire.

Flicker! Flicker! Crackle! Crackle!

"Very good!" said Mrs Pringle, and she chose the Noisy Trio to be the flames... but she didn't choose Daisy.

"Now," called Mrs Pringle, tapping her stick for attention, "I want you to pretend to be woodland creatures, running away from the flames. Listen to the music and watch carefully."

Mrs Pringle ran away from the Noisy Trio like a frightened animal.

Swoosh! Swoosh! Scamper! Scamper!

"I know this is your very first lesson, Daisy,"
Mrs Pringle said, "but I wonder if you would
like to be the Silver Swan?"

Daisy was thrilled. "Me?" she gasped.
"Oh, Mrs Pringle, I'd love to!"

So the ropes were tied round Daisy's waist,
and she swept across the stage.

Daisy's class practised really hard that summer. At the end of term, they put on their special performance of The Silver Swan. Everyone came to see it.

The curtain rose and the musicians began to play.

Swish! Swish! Swish! Swish!

The trees swayed in the breeze. But then the wind grew stronger and stronger.

Suddenly there was a loud crack, as lightning struck the trees and flames leapt around them.

Flicker! Flicker! Crackle! Crackle!

The woodland creatures started to flee.

Swoosh! Swoosh! Scamper! Scamper!

They were terrified and didn't know where to go. Just then the animals looked up. There above them, swooping softly and silently was the Silver Swan. She would lead them to safety.

And Daisy, the little dancer, glided gently before them and led the woodland creatures safely to the Silver Lagoon.

Everyone clapped and cheered and shouted for more.

The musicians and dancers had done so well that Mrs Pringle wanted to cry for joy.

Daisy was the proudest little dancer in the whole ballet school. Perhaps one day she would be famous, after all!